For Gabrielle

Copyright © Text Ann Cartwright 1993
Copyright © Illustrations Reg Cartwright 1993

The rights of Ann and Reg Cartwright to be identified as the
author and illustrator of this work have been asserted by them in
accordance with the Copyright, Designs and Patents Act, 1988.

First published in 1993 by Hutchinson Children's Books
an imprint of Random House UK Limited
20 Vauxhall Bridge Road
London SW1V 2SA

Random House Australia (Pty) Limited
20 Alfred Street, Milsons Point, Sydney,
New South Wales 2061, Australia

Random House New Zealand Limited
18 Poland Road, Glenfield,
Auckland 10, New Zealand

Random House South Africa (Pty) Limited
PO Box 337, Bergvlei, 2012, South Africa

Designed by Paul Welti
Set in Baskerville by Creative Text Limited
Printed in Hong Kong

British Library Cataloguing in Publication Data is available

ISBN 0 09 176427 0

JACKDAW

Story by Ann Cartwright
Illustrations by Reg Cartwright

HUTCHINSON
LONDON SYDNEY AUCKLAND JOHANNESBURG

Once there was a lonely boy. He was shy and found it hard to make friends. But he knew a wonderful secret.

One Saturday he set off on his bicycle. He cycled through the village, into the countryside, and on and on until he came to a field. In the middle of the field stood a tall tree. The tree held the secret that only the boy knew about.

He left his bicycle and climbed into the branches. In the centre of the tree was a hole. He peered inside. There was the treasure – four speckled eggs, warm and snug in the nest.

'Here they are, and still unhatched,' he said.

He picked one up, wrapped it in his handkerchief and put it gently in his pocket. 'The mother bird still has three,' he told himself, 'so she won't miss this one.'

But he knew his parents would be angry if they saw the egg, so he decided to keep it a secret.

When he got home, he crept round the side of the house and down the path to the shed. He made a nest of straw in a plant-pot and gently placed the treasure inside.

'What have you been up to today?' asked his mother later when they were having tea.

'Nothing,' said the boy guiltily. But he felt a tremor of excitement at the thought of the egg lying safe and warm in its new nest.

Lying in bed that night, he wondered what
sort of bird would hatch from the egg.
Perhaps it would be a swallow, a robin, or
even an owl. In the morning he leapt out of
bed and rushed to the shed. A beam of
sunlight shone through the window and lit
up the flowerpot nest.

   Then something miraculous happened. A
crack appeared in the egg, then another,
then another. A tiny claw, fragile as straw,
broke through, then a beak and a head. It
was a baby jackdaw!

   The boy was so excited and proud he
longed to tell someone. But he didn't have
any real friends and his parents would make
him return the baby to its mother.

Then he had an idea. A girl from his
school lived across the road; perhaps
she could keep a secret? He decided to
tell her.

The girl was angry at first and told
him he was cruel to take the egg from
its mother. But she was curious to see
the baby and followed him to the shed.
She was enchanted. The little bird
looked at her with round unblinking
eyes as the boy fed it morsels of food.

Suddenly the boy felt fiercely
protective of the little bird.

'Don't you *ever* tell!' he told the girl.

And she didn't. Weeks passed and as
the bird grew bigger it became restless
and began to flap its wings.

One day the boy opened the door and let the jackdaw hop free. It flew up to the apple tree and examined the garden with bright eyes. The boy held his breath. He was afraid the jackdaw would fly off and be gone forever. But when he held out a bowl of food and cried, 'Jack, Jack!' the young bird flew to him as if he were its mother.

The boy's parents watched from the window. His mother was angry with him for stealing the bird and said he should return it straightaway. But his father was amazed that he had managed to rear the bird all by himself.

'He's a lonely child,' he said. 'The bird will be good for him. Let him keep it.'

And so he did. When the boy walked to school the jackdaw followed him, flying low over the hedges. After school the boy would stand outside the gate and cry, 'Jack, Jack!' and it would fly to him. The lonely boy soon became the centre of attention and everyone wanted to be his friend.

But there was one boy, a big boy, who was jealous. He saw how everyone made a fuss of the bird and began to want it for himself. He offered to swap his penknife for the jackdaw. But the boy said no.

Next day, when the boy went to the shed and called, 'Jack, Jack!' there was no reply. The bird was gone! He searched the garden and ran out into the street. All day long the boy searched for the bird. He felt sick with worry. At lunchtime he wasn't hungry and at teatime he couldn't eat. He wondered if this was how the mother bird had felt when he had stolen her egg, and he felt ashamed.

He went out into the garden. Watching the birds flying free in the sky, he felt a great sadness.

When evening came and the bird still hadn't returned, he telephoned the girl across the road and told her the news.

'Mmmm,' she said. 'I think I can guess what has happened. Meet me outside.'

The boy followed the girl to a house on the edge of the village. It was the house of the boy who had offered the swap. They peered through the garage window. There was the bird, huddled in a corner. Poor thing! It was a sorry sight, its feathers were ruffled and its wings drooped. The boy opened the garage door and softly called, 'Jack, Jack!' It stirred and fluttered into his hands. He caressed it and smoothed its feathers.

The next morning the boy got up early. He found a carton and made some holes in the lid. Then he placed the bird inside and put the carton in his rucksack. He called on the girl across the road and together they cycled to the field. High up in the tall tree another jackdaw called, 'Jack, Jack!' The bird listened.

'Goodbye, Jack,' sang the boy, and he opened the box and let his bird fly free. 'Goodbye.'

The jackdaw flew up into the air and from the tree flew the other jackdaw. The pair flew higher and higher and higher until they were no more than specks in the sky.